Captain Wobbly and the Invasion from Erm

written by Laura Carter
illustrated by Gary Andrews

LC: "For my son Tomos, because there is a space ship in this one."

GA: "For my amazing wife Joy, who makes everything possible."

WOBBLY
HEAD →

WOBBLY
ELBOWS

WOBBLY
KNEES

WOBBLY
TOES

Captain Wobbly (AKA Ricky Maloney)

ULTRA SLEEK
SPOILER

SOME
LIGHT
READING

RETRO
FIT
TURBO

RACING
TYRES

WELL COOL
PAINT JOB

Cool Stevie

Joanne

AMAZING
HAIR

WINNING
SMILE

ULTRACALC
5000

GREAT
FASHION
SENSE

Our story starts on holiday in beautiful West Wales
On craggy cliffs, white beaches and leafy forest trails.

5

The wobbliest of heroes with the wobbliest of knees,
Was rambling with his pals (the twins), cape flapping in the breeze.

Cool Steve was navigating using inbuilt Sat Nav Tech
His off-road tyres were knobbly and the latest, highest spec.

At once Joanne leapt forward, her red curls bouncing free...

"What on Earth's that object, suspended out to sea?"

And then there came the chaos, Her Majesty's bold troops
Came swarming in with speedboats and choppers doing loops.
The UFO, surrounded with military might,
Managed to look nervous, and lowered hovering height.

A beam of light shot skyward, then darted and aimed low.
The air around them crackled and it landed next to Jo.

"ErrrrrrrrrrrrrrrrrrrrrrrrmmmmmmmmmmmbzzzzzzzzzzzzzzzPOP!"
The alien visitor said.
He offered do a tentacle and politely bowed his head.

"How d'ya do?" Said Ricky. Jo exclaimed "Good Lord!"
"Hand's up!" yelled Colonel Whittington, brandishing a sword.

The alien squealed loudly and leapt into the air
Displaying some strange movements and colour changing hair.

"By Gad!" the Colonel shouted, "Let's shoot the blighter, quick!"

But Ricky spotted something and shouted "Wait a tick!"

13

"I know that jazzy dancing, they're some retro vintage moves
Circa 1983 - they were such classic grooves!"

"Ah ha!" Joanne expounded from her super science book
"The Spitzer Telescope has spotted something.
                                        Take a look!"

"There is an exoplanet, its year is one Earth day.
It's orbiting a red dwarf, 33 light years away.

He's seen our TV signals, thinks *that's* how we relate.
He's watched some vintage pop programmes but 33 years late!"

"What rubbish!" sneered the Colonel, "I've never heard such tosh!"
He swung his sword towards the sea (it landed with a splosh!).

The alien looked worried and slid behind Joanne.
The Captain ruefully pondered and came up with a plan.

He got into position, held his arms up high
Performed the 'Macarena' while the army looked awry

The alien smiled widely, his tentacles full span
He paused and, with high drama, performed the 'Running Man'.

Then he reached into a pocket, to the Colonel's perturbations
(He wasn't really after interstellar type relations).

The alien withdrew a map and pointed with a growl.
"He wants to visit Cardiff but the signposts have no vowels!"

At once cool Steve came forward and offered up his tech
The creature tapped the postcode in and rubbed his stripy neck.

Cool Stevie raised one eyebrow, a glint in his left eye
He pressed a bright red button and his chair flew in the sky.

It whirred and clicked and shuddered. Out sideways slid the wheels
"Jump on!" asserted Joanne, "Let's see how flying feels!"

The rocket boosters rumbled and shot out tongues of fire
The passengers hung on for life, the chair ascended higher.

"To Cardiff!" Ricky shouted,
"You won't see us for dust!"
The army took some pot-shots,
Cool Stevie increased thrust.

The chair began to sputter.
Steve went to dive too steep.
He closed his eyes and pulled up hard,
frightening some sheep...

Joanne did some adjustments,
Stevie gained control,
He got a bit too confident
and did a barrel roll.

26

"Look, it's Cardiff Castle!", and Stevie swooped down lower.
"Quick, let's land and get ourselves a selfie on the tower..."

27

They landed on a turret and looked out at the view.
Joanne took out some Chewy Mints and handed out a few.

The friends admired the sunset.
Waved at the castle guard.
The alien took out a pen and
wrote a space postcard.

So all you youngsters out there, a lesson learnt today:
When Dad's or Auntie Phyllis's hips begin to sway...

Don't take the mick or giggle. Those ancient moves; don't shun.
For one day you might need them all to greet an alien!

Hi, I'm Laura, and I write because I want my kids to be able to read books about other kids having fabulous adventures, no matter what their ability is. Wobbly kids, kids with wheels, kids who communicate in a different way - they all need role models too.

My stories have been brought into glorious life by the amazing Gary Andrews, who uses his magic to create a colour and movement which is nothing short of genius.

Hello there! I'm Gary and have been drawing ever since I could hold a pencil. I went to Exeter Art College where I specialised in illustration and from where I graduated in 1983. I'm still drawing!

I was honoured to be asked by Laura to illustrate her books, as I think she has a funny and original vision. I hope you are drawn into her world, just as I was...